Nursery
Stories

Mallard Press and its accompanying design and logo
are trademarks of BDD Promotional Book Company, Inc.
First published in the United States of America
in 1991 by The Mallard Press.
First published in the U.K. by Kingfisher Books.
Text copyright © Susan Price 1990
Illustrations copyright © Colin and Moira Maclean 1990

ISBN 0-792-45493-6
Printed in Spain

Nursery Stories

A collection of traditional favorites
for the very young

SELECTED AND RETOLD BY
SUSAN PRICE

ILLUSTRATED BY
COLIN AND MOIRA MACLEAN

MALLARD
PRESS

CONTENTS

Goldilocks and the Three Bears

Once upon a time, deep in a dark wood, lived three bears.

The biggest was Daddy Bear. The middling one was Mummy Bear. And the littlest one was Baby Bear. They all lived together in a little house and they were happy.

Every morning they had porridge for breakfast. But one morning the porridge was too hot and burned their mouths. "Let's go for a walk in the wood," said Mummy Bear, "until the porridge is cool enough to eat."

"Good idea," said Daddy Bear. So they took Baby Bear's paws in theirs, and walked out in the wood.

The little house was left empty, with three bowls of porridge cooling on the table.

Then, through the wood came a little girl. She was lost and hungry, and her name was Goldilocks.

When she saw the little house she thought, "Oh, I wonder who lives there. Perhaps they can tell me how to find my way out of the wood. Perhaps they can give me something to eat." So she went up to the door of the little house and knocked.

But no one came to the door, even when she knocked again.

She tried to look in at the window, but she wasn't tall enough.

She called, but still no one came.

So she stood on tip-toe, and stretched up high, and opened the door, even though it wasn't her house! She went quietly inside and looked around.

No one was at home. But on the table stood those three bowls of porridge: a great big bowl, a middling-sized bowl, and a tiny little bowl.

"I'm so hungry," thought Goldilocks, "and there's no one here to ask. I'll just try this porridge."

First she went to the great big bowl. She dug in the spoon and took a big mouthful. But it was HOT!

"Too hot! Too hot!" said Goldilocks, and she dropped the spoon back in the bowl.

She went to the middling-sized bowl and tried a spoonful of that. But it was sticky and COLD. Goldilocks made a face. "Too cold! Too cold!" she said.

And she dropped the spoon back in the bowl.

Then she tried the porridge in the littlest bowl. It was not too hot and not too cold, but just right! So she ate it all up and licked the bowl clean.

Now Goldilocks was tired because she'd walked so far through the wood. She saw three chairs against the wall: a big chair, a middling-sized chair, and a tiny little chair.

First she climbed onto the great big chair, but it was too hard, and she slid off again.

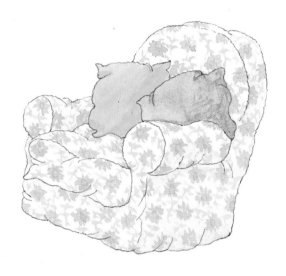

Then Goldilocks tried the middling-sized chair, but that was too soft, and she soon scrambled off.

But when she sat in the tiny little chair, it wasn't too hard and it wasn't too soft. It was just right, so she thought, "I'll sit here for a while."

But just as Goldilocks thought that, the tiny little chair broke, and she fell on the floor!

When she got up she was cross, and still tired. So she went upstairs, even though it wasn't her house, and found a room with three beds in it.

There was a great big bed, a middling-sized bed, and a tiny little bed.

Goldilocks tried the great big bed first, but it was too hard. So she rolled off it and tried the middling-sized bed, but it was too soft.

So she left that one and tried the tiny little bed. Now that bed wasn't too hard and it wasn't too soft. It was just right! Goldilocks fell fast asleep.

While she was asleep, the three bears came home from their walk in the wood. They looked at their por- ridge bowls, and Daddy Bear saw that a big spoonful had been taken from his bowl.

15

In his great big bear's voice, he growled, "Who's been eating my porridge?"

In her soft, middling voice, Mummy Bear said, "And who's been eating my porridge?"

In her tiny little voice, Baby Bear said, "Who's been eating my porridge, and has eaten it all up?"

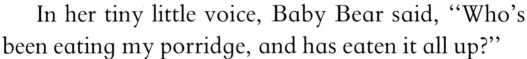Then Daddy Bear saw that his chair had been moved and he roared, "Who's been sitting on my chair?"

And Mummy Bear said, "Who's been sitting on my chair?"

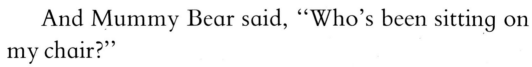Baby Bear began to cry, "Who's been sitting in my chair, and has broken it all up?"

Then the three bears went upstairs. In his great big voice, Daddy Bear said, "Who's been sleeping in my bed?"

And Mummy Bear said, "Who's been sleeping in my bed?"

Then Baby Bear cried, "Who's been sleeping in my bed and is still in it?"

Mummy Bear and Daddy Bear came to look. There lay Goldilocks, snoring in the little bed. But the sound of Baby Bear crying woke her, and she sat up.

When she saw three bears looking at her, she was so frightened that she jumped right out of the window. Luckily she landed in soft grass, so she wasn't hurt. She ran and ran and ran. Soon she was out of the wood, and then she knew her way home. Goldilocks never came back, and lived happily ever after.

As for the three bears, whenever they went for a walk after that, they remembered to lock their door, so no one could creep in, eat their porridge, or break their chairs. So they lived happily ever after too. Everyone was happy. And that's the end.

The Three Little Pigs

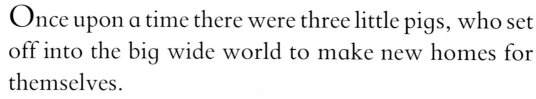

Once upon a time there were three little pigs, who set off into the big wide world to make new homes for themselves.

The first little pig was walking along the road when he met a man carrying a load of straw. "Straw," thought the little pig. "I could easily build a house of straw. It wouldn't take long, or be much trouble."

So the first little pig bought the load of straw from the man, and built himself a house with it. And he lived happily in his house of straw.

The second little pig was walking along the road when he met a man carrying a load of sticks. "Sticks," thought the little pig. "I could easily build a house of sticks. It wouldn't take long, or be much trouble."

So the second little pig bought the sticks from the man, and built himself a house with them. And he lived happily in his house of sticks.

The third little pig was walking along the road when he met a man with a load of bricks. "Bricks," thought the little pig. "I could build a house of bricks. It would take a long time, and a lot of trouble, but when it was finished, it would be a good strong house."

So the third little pig bought the bricks from the man, and he set to work to build himself a brick house. It took him many weeks of mixing mortar to stick the bricks together, and of laying the bricks one on top of another to make the walls. Day after day he worked away at it.

The first little pig and the second little pig often came to watch. "Look at you, working so hard!" they said. "We finished our houses long ago, and now we can play."

"Yes," said the third little pig, "but my house will be drier than yours, and warmer and stronger."

But the first little pig and the second little pig didn't think that mattered. They laughed and ran away.

Then came the big bad wolf. Wolves eat little pigs.

The big bad wolf saw the first little pig, and the first little pig saw him.

Away ran the little pig, and shut himself into his house of straw.

"Let me in, little pig, let me in," said the wolf.

"Oh, no, not by the hair of my chinny-chin-chin!" said the little pig. "I won't let you in."

"Then I'll huff, and I'll puff, and I'll blow your house down!" said the wolf.

And the wolf huffed, and he puffed, and he blew down the house of straw. And if the first little pig hadn't been quick, he would have been eaten. But he was quick, and he ran away to the house of sticks where his brother lived.

The two little pigs shut themselves into the house of sticks, and waited. By and by the wolf came, and the wolf said, "Let me in, little pigs, let me in."

"Oh no, not by the hairs on our chinny-chin-chins, we won't let you in," said the two little pigs.

"Then I'll huff, and I'll puff, and I'll blow your house down!" said the wolf.

And he huffed, and he puffed, and he blew down the house of sticks. And if the two little pigs hadn't been quick, they would have been eaten. But they were quick, and they ran away to the house of bricks where their brother lived.

The three little pigs shut themselves into the house of bricks. By and by the wolf came, and said, "Let me in, little pigs, let me in."

"Oh no, not by the hairs on our chinny-chin-chins, we won't let you in," said the three little pigs.

"Then I'll huff, and I'll puff, and I'll blow your house down!" said the wolf.

He huffed, and he puffed—but the house of bricks didn't fall down.

So the wolf took a bigger breath, and he huffed harder and puffed harder—but the house of bricks still didn't fall down.

So the wolf took an even deeper breath, and he huffed harder still, and puffed harder still, but the house of bricks just wouldn't fall down, because it was stronger than straw or sticks.

The wolf was exhausted with huffing and puffing, and he crawled away to get his breath back.

The first little pig and the second little pig cheered, because they thought that they were safe now. But the third little pig said, "Help me to fill the cooking pot with water and light a fire under it."

So they lit a fire and they hung the big cooking pot over it, and they filled the pot with water. The water was soon boiling. "That wolf won't have given up yet," said the third little pig. "We have to be ready for him."

The wolf got his breath back, and wondered how he could get the little pigs. He couldn't blow down the brick house because it was too strong. He couldn't get in by the door because it was locked. He couldn't get in by the windows because they were shuttered. But there was the chimney.

So the wolf climbed up onto the roof, and climbed down the chimney to get the three little pigs.

But he landed right in the cooking pot that the three little pigs had ready. Instead of the wolf having pig for his dinner, the three little pigs had wolf stew for theirs.

Then the first little pig and the second little pig built brick houses for themselves, and they all lived happily ever after. And that's the end of the story.

The Gingerbread Man

Once upon a time, there was an old woman who was baking. She made a gingerbread man for tea. She cut him out of spicy gingerbread and gave him currants for his eyes and mouth and currant buttons down his front. Then she put him in the oven to bake.

A little while later, there was a knock at the door. Not the kitchen door—the oven door! A voice shouted, "Let me out! Let me out!"

So the old woman opened the oven door and *whoosh!* the gingerbread man raced past her, across the kitchen floor and out into the garden. The old woman ran after him, shouting, "Come back! I baked you for tea!"

But the gingerbread man only laughed and ran on, calling, "Run, run, as fast as you can—you won't catch me, I'm the gingerbread man!"

The old woman's husband was digging in the garden, and he blinked when he saw the gingerbread man run past. Then he saw his wife running after him and heard her shouting, "Stop that gingerbread man! He's for our tea!" So the old man dropped his

spade, and he ran after the gingerbread man too.

"Stop!" he shouted. "You're for my tea!"

But the gingerbread man only laughed. "Your wife can't catch me and nor will you! Run, run, as fast as you can—you'll never catch me, I'm the gingerbread man!"

And he ran on, down the road, with the old man and the old woman panting after him.

He ran past a cow, and the cow smelled the spicy gingerbread. "Mmm!" said the cow. "Come back, I want to eat you."

But the gingerbread man only laughed. "The old woman can't catch me, nor the old man. And no cow in the world can! Run, run, as fast as you can—you won't catch me, I'm the gingerbread man!"

And on he ran. The cow came lumbering after him, and panting along behind the cow came the old man and the old woman, all three of them chasing the runaway gingerbread man.

The gingerbread man ran past a horse, and the horse smelled the spicy gingerbread. "Hey!" said the horse. "Come back! I'd like to eat you!"

But the gingerbread man only laughed. "The old woman can't catch me, nor the old man; the cow can't

catch me, and no horse in the world can! Run, run, as fast as you can—you won't catch me, I'm the gingerbread man!"

And on he ran. After him the horse came galloping, and behind the horse the cow came lumbering, and panting along behind the cow came the old man and the old woman, all of them chasing the runaway gingerbread man.

Then the gingerbread man ran past some haymakers who were working in a field. The haymakers smelled the spicy gingerbread and said, "Ooh! Come back, gingerbread man! We'd like to eat you!"

But the gingerbread man only laughed and said, "The old woman can't catch me, nor the old man; the cow can't, the horse can't, and no one in the world can! So run, run, as fast as you can—you won't catch me, I'm the gingerbread man!"

And on he ran; and after him ran all the haymakers, shouting; and behind them came the horse, galloping; and behind them, the cow, lumbering; and behind them, the old man and the old woman, panting. All of them chasing the runaway gingerbread man.

But ahead of the gingerbread man was a wide, deep river. By the edge of the river sat a fox, watching everything.

The gingerbread man had to stop when he reached the river. He couldn't go into the water, or he would melt.

"Now what are you going to do?" asked the fox.

The gingerbread man was afraid of the fox, but he still said, "Run, run, as fast as you can—you won't catch me, I'm the gingerbread man!"

"I don't want to run," said the fox, "and I don't want to catch you. I never eat gingerbread—it's bad for my teeth. Would you like me to carry you across the river?"

"You won't eat me?" asked the gingerbread man.

"You can sit on my tail, which is farthest from my mouth. I can't eat you then, can I?" said the clever fox.

The gingerbread man got onto the fox's tail and the fox started to swim across. The hay-makers, the horse, the cow, the old man, and the old woman all ran down to the river bank, too late. The gingerbread man waved to them from the fox's tail and shouted, "Run, run, as fast as you can—you won't catch me, I'm the gingerbread man!"

As the fox swam across the river, his tail got wet, so the gingerbread man climbed a little farther up to the fox's back.

As the fox swam on, the river got deeper, and more and more of his back was under water. The gingerbread man had to move up farther, onto the fox's shoulders. But soon even the fox's shoulders were wet.

"Climb onto my head," said the fox. "You'll be dry there."

So the gingerbread man climbed up onto the fox's head. But soon even the fox's head got splashed. Only his nose was poking above the surface.

"Climb onto my nose," said the fox. "You'll be dry there."

So the gingerbread man climbed onto the fox's

nose. Just as the fox reached the other side of the river, and was climbing out onto the bank, he gave his nose a quick *flip!* Up into the air sailed the gingerbread man. The fox opened his mouth wide. Down fell the gingerbread man, right into the fox's mouth —SNAP!

The fox sat on the bank and looked at the haymakers, the horse, the cow, the old man, and the old woman on the other side. He liked his lips and said, "Run, run, as fast as you can—it takes a fox to catch a gingerbreadman!"

Foxes are clever; they know that it takes more to catch a gingerbread man than running after them shouting, "Come back! I want to eat you!"

32

The Little Red Hen

Once upon a time, in a farmyard, there lived a little red hen with her chicks. She was always scratching around, always busy.

A dog, a cat, and a pig lived in the farmyard too. But they were lazy. The dog slept nearly all day, the cat slept even longer, and the pig was always either eating or lying in his mud patch.

One day, the little red hen found a grain of wheat. "Who will help me plant this grain?" she asked.

"Not I," said the dog.

"Not I," said the cat.

"Not I," said the pig. They were all too idle.

"Then I shall do it, and my chicks will help me," said the little red hen. She scratched a hole in the earth and planted the grain of wheat, and her chicks helped her.

But the sun was hot and baked the earth so hard that the wheat couldn't grow.

"Who will help me water the wheat?" asked the little red hen.

"Not I," said the dog.

"Not I," said the cat.

"Not I," said the pig.

"Then I shall do it, and my chicks will help me," said the little red hen. She carried water from the pump and watered the wheat, and her chicks helped her.

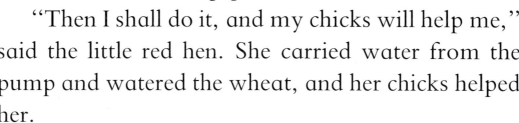

After that, the wheat grew and grew. First it was green, then it turned yellow, and now it was ready to be harvested.

"Who will help me harvest the wheat?" asked the little red hen.

"Not I," said the dog.

"Not I," said the cat.

"Not I," said the pig.

"Then I shall do it, and my chicks will help me." And she and her chicks cut down the wheat.

To separate the good grain from the husk, the wheat had to be threshed and winnowed. "Who will help me thresh the wheat?" asked the little red hen.

"Not I," said the dog.

"Not I," said the cat.

"Not I," said the pig.

"Then I shall do it," said the little red hen, "and my chicks will help me." She and her chicks worked hard threshing the wheat and throwing it into the air for the husks to blow away.

"Who will help me carry the grain to the mill, to have it ground into flour?" asked the little red hen.

"Not I," said the dog.

"Not I," said the cat.

"Not I," said the pig.

"Then I shall do it, and my chicks will help me." The little red hen and her chicks carried the grain all the way to the mill. When it was ground, they carried the flour all the way home.

"Now, who will help me bake a cake?" asked the little red hen.

"Not I," said the dog.

"Not I," said the cat.

"Not I," said the pig.

"Then I'll bake it myself," said the little red hen, "and my chicks will help me." She set to work and baked a cake, and her chicks helped her. When the cake was ready, the little red hen took it out of the

oven. A beautiful, sweet, spicy, warm smell drifted over the farmyard. The dog lifted his head and sniffed. The cat twitched her nose and sniffed. The pig sat up in his mud patch and sniffed.

"Who will help me eat this cake?" asked the little red hen.

"I will!" said the dog.

"And I will!" said the cat.

"Me too!" said the pig.

"Oh no you won't!" said the little red hen. "Not a slice, not a crumb. My chicks and I did all the work, so my chicks and I shall eat all the cake!"

They did, and a fine cake it was. Now all the cake is finished, and so is this story.

The Three Billy Goats Gruff

Once upon a time, there were three billy goats: Little Billy Goat Gruff, Middle-Sized Billy Goat Gruff, and Great Big Billy Goat Gruff. They'd been shut in a shed all winter, with nothing to eat but hay, and they were thin. In the spring they were let out of their shed. Off they went to the mountain meadows, to eat the sweet, new, juicy, spring grass.

"You two go ahead," said Great Big Billy Goat Gruff. "There's a thistle or two here I mean to eat before I go on."

So Middle-Sized Billy Goat Gruff and Little Billy Goat Gruff went on without him.

Then, "You go on ahead," said Middle-Sized Billy Goat Gruff to Little Billy Goat Gruff. "There's just one or two leaves on this thorn–bush I mean to eat before I go on."

So Little Billy Goat Gruff went on alone.

To reach the mountain meadow where the sweet, new, juicy, spring grass grew, Little Billy Goat Gruff had to cross a wooden bridge over a high waterfall. Under the bridge lived a troll; a horrible, howling,

38

gobbling, greedy troll. As Little Billy Goat Gruff crossed the bridge, his little hooves went trip-trip-trip on the wooden planks. The troll underneath heard, and yelled out, "Who's trip-tripping across my bridge?"

"It's only me," said Little Billy Goat Gruff. "I'm just going to get fat on the sweet, new, juicy, spring grass over there in the meadow."

The troll was furious. He jumped up onto the bridge and landed in front of Little Billy Goat Gruff.

"Nobody crosses *my* bridge!" he yelled. "I'm going to eat you, little goat. I'm going to eat you from your horns to your heels."

"Oh, please don't eat me, you wouldn't enjoy me!" said Little Billy Goat Gruff. "I'm so small and skinny, I'd hardly be a mouthful for you. Wait for my brother, Middle-Sized Billy Goat Gruff. He'd make a much better meal."

The troll thought about it. "You *are* skinny," he said. "Hardly worth chewing. Yes, get off my bridge! I'll wait for your brother."

Little Billy Goat Gruff ran quickly across the bridge, trip-trip-trip, and was soon among the sweet,

new, juicy, spring grass on the other side, eating as much as he could.

The troll went back under the bridge and waited.

Soon Middle-Sized Billy Goat Gruff had finished the leaves on the thorn-bush and came across the bridge. His middle-sized hooves went trot-trot-trot on the wooden planks. The troll underneath heard, and yelled out, "Who's trot-trotting across my bridge?"

"Only me," said Middle-Sized Billy Goat Gruff. "I'm going to the meadow, to eat the sweet, new, juicy, spring grass."

Up onto the bridge jumped the troll. He was furious. "Nobody crosses *my* bridge," he screamed. "I'm going to eat you, every scrap of you, from your horns to your heels. That'll teach you to trot-trot your nasty hooves across *my* bridge."

"You don't want to eat me," said Middle-Sized Billy Goat Gruff. "I'm not nearly big enough to fill your belly."

"You're bigger than your skinny little brother," said the troll.

"Yes," said Middle-Sized Billy Goat Gruff, "but I'm not nearly as big as our brother, Great Big Billy Goat Gruff. He's twice as big as me. Now *he* would make a meal fit for a troll."

The troll thought about it. "You're right," he said. "It makes sense to wait for the biggest of you. Get off my bridge then, before I eat you anyway!"

Middle-Sized Billy Goat Gruff ran quickly across the bridge and reached the meadow where his brother Little Billy Goat Gruff was eating the sweet, new, juicy, spring grass.

Soon Great Big Billy Goat Gruff had finished his thistles, so he started across the wooden bridge to join his brothers. Tramp, tramp, tramp went his great big hooves on the wooden planks. Underneath the troll was listening and roared, "Who's tramp-tramping across my bridge?"

"I am," said Great Big Billy Goat Gruff. "I'm going to join my brothers in the meadow and we're all going to get fat."

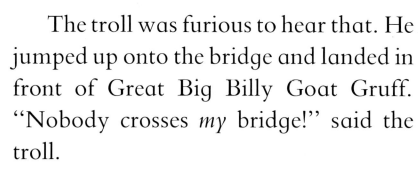

The troll was furious to hear that. He jumped up onto the bridge and landed in front of Great Big Billy Goat Gruff. "Nobody crosses *my* bridge!" said the troll.

"I'm crossing it," said Great Big Billy Goat Gruff.

"No you're not!" screamed the troll. "I'm going to eat you up, horns, hair, and heels—you're going to fill my belly until it feels as if I've eaten half the world. I'm going to—"

"Come and try!" said Great Big Billy Goat Gruff. He lowered his big-horned head and said:

"On my head are two sharp spears;
With them I'll make you cry salt tears!
On my head are two big stones:
I'll thump you hard and smash your
    bones!"

Then he charged at the troll and speared him, thumped him, and tossed him right over the sun and moon. High in the air soared the troll, then down, down, down he fell.

But he didn't land on the bridge—he missed the bridge altogether and fell even farther, down, down, down the waterfall until SPLASH! that was the end of the troll.

Great Big Billy Goat Gruff crossed the bridge, tramp, tramp, tramp, and joined his brothers in the meadow on the other side. They all got fat eating the sweet, new, juicy, spring grass. For all I know, they're still there, growing fatter and fatter every day.

And that's all I know of them, because snip, snap, snout, this tale's told out.

The Magic Porridge Pot

There was once a little girl who lived with her mother. They had no money, and couldn't buy anything to eat. They were hungry all the time.

One day, all the mother had to give the little girl for her dinner was one thin biscuit. "Make it last," said the mother.

The little girl was playing in the street when along came a thin old man. "I haven't tasted a single mouthful in three days," he said. "Can you give me something to eat?"

The little girl gave him her biscuit, because she felt so sorry for him.

"You are kind," said the old man, "and I am going to give you a present." From the pack on his back, he took a little iron pot. "This is a magic pot. It won't work for me, but it will for you. When you want to eat, say 'Little pot, cook!' and it will fill itself with porridge. When you've eaten all you want, say 'Little pot, enough!' and it will stop."

The little girl ran home with the pot, and put it on the table. She called her mother and said, "Little pot, cook!"

Straight away the little pot filled with hot porridge, already mixed with milk and sugar. The little girl and her mother ate three bowls each and felt full and happy. Then the little girl said, "Little pot, enough!" and the pot stopped making porridge.

The girl and her mother were never hungry after that.

But one day the little girl was out playing and the mother wanted some porridge. "I won't call her in," she thought. "I know what to say." And she said "Cook, little pot!"

Nothing happened.

"Oh, wrong way round. Little pot, cook!"

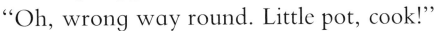
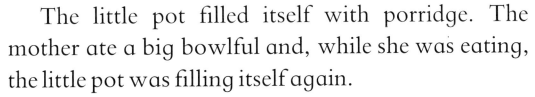

The little pot filled itself with porridge. The mother ate a big bowlful and, while she was eating, the little pot was filling itself again.

The mother didn't want any more, so she said, "Stop, little pot!"

The pot went on filling—and it filled quickly!

"Little pot, stop!"

Porridge began running over the top of the pot.

"Little pot, no more!"

Porridge poured from the pot, over the table, and onto the floor.

"No more, little pot!"

The floor was ankle-deep in gooey porridge.

"Oh what are the right words? Porridge pot, stop!"

Faster and faster came the porridge, rising up the walls, burying the chairs. The mother opened the door and the porridge began running down the street.

"Stop, porridge pot!"

But nothing the mother could think of to say stopped the porridge. It poured down the street and swept a cat off its feet. It ran into other houses and clogged the wheels of cars and bicycles. Porridge everywhere!

The little girl was coming home when she saw a stream of porridge coming toward her carrying along cats and dogs and babies. She guessed what had happened.

She shouted, "Little pot, enough!"

The pot heard her and stopped.

Then everyone had to bring spoons and eat themselves into house and home.

The Lion and the Mouse

A lion was once sleeping in the sun when a mouse ran over his paw and woke him. The lion reached out his paw and caught the mouse by the tail.

The mouse squeaked with fright. "Oh, don't kill me please! Let me go, and I'll do you a good turn one day."

"You're too small ever to be able to do me a good turn," said the lion. "I'll let you go, but only because you're too small to be worth eating."

He lifted his paw and the mouse ran away.

That very night the lion walked into a trap set by hunters. A net made of strong rope fell over him. He couldn't move. Soon the hunters would come and kill him.

But then he heard a squeak, and saw the mouse he had allowed to go free. With sharp little teeth, she began to bite through the ropes. At last all the ropes were chewed right through, and the lion was free.

"I was wrong," said the lion. "I thought you were too small to be of any use to anyone, little mouse, but you have saved my life."

After that the lion remembered that even the small and weak can be of help, even to the strongest.

Jack and the Beanstalk

Once upon a time there was a poor widow who had one son, and his name was Jack. Jack was no help to his mother, because he was lazy and only wanted to lie in front of the fire all day. "You never do anything," she always said to him. "And when you do, you never do it right!"

They had no money at all, and the only thing they had was their old cow. One day Jack's mother said, "Jack, take the old cow to market and sell her for the highest price you can get."

It was a long walk to market, and Jack didn't want to go, but he had no choice. He tied a rope around the old cow's neck and set off, as slowly as he could.

He hadn't gone very far when he met a man. "That's a stringy old thing of a cow," the man said. "Where are you taking her?"

"To market, to sell her," said Jack.

"You won't get much for that old thing," said the man. "How much are you asking for her?"

"How much are you offering?" asked Jack.

The man put his hand in his pocket and pulled something out. "Five beans—and you won't get any more for that old creature at market!"

"That may be," said Jack, "but my mother will be furious if I go home with nothing but five beans. Even five pennies would be better."

"But these are magic beans," said the man. "They will make your fortune."

"Done!" said Jack, because he really couldn't be bothered to walk all the way to market. So the man gave him the five beans and Jack gave the man the cow, and then went home.

"Back already?" said his mother. "What did you get for the cow?"

Jack took the beans from his pocket and showed them to his mother. "Beans!" she said. "Five beans! Why, you useless great lump!" She threw the beans out of the window. Then she sent Jack to bed. He didn't even get a chance to explain that the beans were magic and would make their fortune.

When Jack woke up the next morning, the house was dark, as if it were still night. Something was blocking the window.

Jack ran outside and saw a huge beanstalk that grew up and up until it disappeared into the clouds. "They *were* magic beans," Jack said to himself. "I wonder what's up there." He started to climb the beanstalk, to find out what was at the top.

Jack climbed up and up and up, all the way to the top. There he found a path, leading through the clouds to a great big castle.

Jack knocked on the door. A huge woman opened it. She looked surprised to see him. "What are you doing here?" she asked. "Don't you know that a giant lives here, a giant who eats boys?"

Jack said, "But I've climbed so high and walked so far. I'm hungry—thirsty too."

"Come in," said the woman. "But you mustn't stay long."

Inside the castle, Jack and the woman got talking. Before they knew it, noisy footsteps were coming up the path.

"It's my husband, the giant!" said the woman. "Quick! Hide!"

Jack jumped into an empty pot by the stove and pulled down the lid.

The door opened and in came the giant. He sniffed the air and said,

"Fee, fi, fo, fum,

I smell the blood of an Englishman.

Be he alive or be he dead,

I'll grind his bones to make my bread!"

"How you go on," said the giant's wife. "There's no one here. Now sit down and eat your dinner."

So the giant sat down and ate his dinner. Then he took out a grubby-looking purse, opened it and tipped it upside down. Out fell a great heap of gold. The giant closed the purse, opened it again—and it was filled with gold once more!

Jack was peeping out of his pot and saw. "If my mother and I had that purse," he thought, "we'd never be poor again." He made up his mind that he was going to take that purse home with him, come what may.

He watched and waited until the giant went over to his chair in front of the fire, kicked off his boots and went to sleep. Then Jack crept out of the pot, grabbed the purse—and ran for his life!

Out of the castle he ran, along the path, down the beanstalk and into his house, shouting, "Mother! Mother! Look!"

Jack's mother was amazed that her lazy son Jack had done such a brave thing. She looked at the purse and said, "Now we shall never be poor again. So promise me that you won't climb the beanstalk any more. It's dangerous."

Jack promised he wouldn't.

With the money that the purse gave them, they were much happier than before, but Jack couldn't forget the castle. One day, while his mother was out, he climbed the beanstalk again.

When Jack knocked on the castle door, the giant's wife opened it and said, "You again! If the giant finds you here—well, he'll eat you raw!"

"Oh, I'll be long gone before he gets back," Jack said. "But I must have a sit down and something to eat and drink. I've come such a long way."

The kind woman took him in. Jack wanted to stay until the giant came home, so he got her talking until she forgot all about the time passing.

Then they heard the giant coming home.

Jack opened the cupboard under the sink and crawled inside. In came the giant, sniffing the air.

"Fee, fi, fo, fum,
I smell the blood of an Englishman.
Be he alive or be he dead,
I'll have his blood to sauce my bread!"

"Oh, don't go on so," said the giant's wife. "There's no one here. Eat your dinner, you big lump."

So the giant sat down to his dinner. When he'd finished, he brought out a beautiful red hen. He stroked her feathers gently and the hen laid eggs for him. Not ordinary eggs, but eggs of beautiful shining gold!

Jack waited until the giant had fallen asleep by the fire. Then he crept out of the cupboard, grabbed the hen—and ran for his life!

Out of the castle, along the path, down the beanstalk, and into his house he ran, shouting. "Mother! Mother! Look!"

When Jack's mother saw the hen and the eggs, she could hardly believe her eyes. She made him promise, *promise*, never to climb the beanstalk again.

Jack promised.

With all the gold from the purse, and the golden eggs from the hen, they were rich. But Jack couldn't forget the castle. He climbed the beanstalk again.

When the giant's wife opened the door and saw who it was, she said, "Go away! I dare not let you in." But she was a kind woman, and Jack persuaded her to let him in after all. They got talking, and the giant's wife soon forgot all about the time—until she heard her husband coming home.

Jack crawled under the washtub and hid.

In came the giant, sniffing the air.

"Fee, fi, fo, fum,

I smell the blood of an Englishman ..."

"Oh, get away with you," said his wife. "Sit down and have your dinner."

When the giant had eaten his dinner, he fetched a beautiful golden harp. "Play, harp," he said, and the harp played beautiful music, all by itself!

Jack waited until the giant fell asleep by the fire, crept out, grabbed the harp—and ran for his life!

But as he ran, the harp cried out, "Master! Master!" The giant woke up, jumped to his feet and ran after Jack with great big strides.

Jack reached the beanstalk first, and started climbing down as fast as he could. But the giant reached the beanstalk too, and began climbing down after Jack.

Jack reached the ground first, dropped the harp and snatched up an ax his mother used to chop wood. He began to chop down the beanstalk.

He chopped and chopped and chopped, and at last he chopped right through. Down came the beanstalk, and down came the giant. With a CRASH! the giant landed on his head, and that was the end of him.

So Jack and his mother had the purse of gold, and the hen that laid golden eggs, and the harp that played all by itself, and they lived happily in comfort all the rest of their lives.

And that is the end of the story.

The Elves and the Shoemaker

Once upon a time there was a poor shoemaker. He was a good shoemaker, but there were many other shoemakers in the town, and no matter how hard he worked, he couldn't sell enough shoes to feed his family. Soon he had only one small bit of leather left, and no money to buy any more.

"Without leather, I can't make shoes," he said to his wife. "And if I can't make shoes, I can't sell any. And if I don't sell any shoes, we shan't have any money to buy food. We shall go hungry, you and our children and I."

"Well," said his wife, "make one last pair of shoes with that last bit of leather."

The shoemaker did as his wife said, and cut out the pieces. He didn't have time to sew the shoes together that night, so he left the pieces lying on his workbench.

The next morning, when he came back to his workbench to finish the shoes, he found they'd already been finished! There on the workbench was a beautiful pair of shoes! He picked them up and looked

at them. The stitches were so tiny they couldn't be seen. The seams were so smooth they would never rub. They were the best pair of shoes the shoemaker had ever seen.

"But how did they get here?" he asked himself. "Who made them?"

Since the shoes *were* there, and since they were so fine, the shoemaker put them in his shop window. A rich gentleman came in and bought them right away—for more money than the shoemaker had ever been paid before.

The shoemaker's wife was able to buy food for the family, and the shoemaker bought more leather to make more shoes. All day long he worked, cutting

60

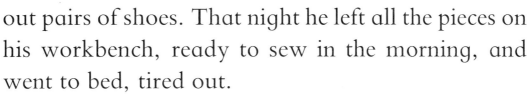

out pairs of shoes. That night he left all the pieces on his workbench, ready to sew in the morning, and went to bed, tired out.

The next morning, the shoemaker came back to his workbench and found that all his work had been done for him, again! All the pieces he had left on his bench the night before had been sewn together, much more cleverly than the shoemaker himself could have done it. The shoemaker put the shoes in his window, and by that night he had sold them all, for good prices.

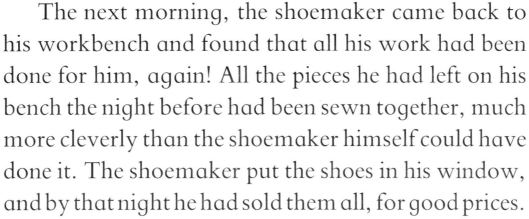

And so it went on. The shoemaker cut out shoes during the day; and during the night someone came and sewed them together. The shoemaker didn't know who was doing the work, but whoever it was, there wasn't a better shoemaker in town.

Soon everyone was coming to the shop to buy their shoes. The shoemaker was famous. And he was rich.

Just before Christmas, the shoemaker had an idea. "Wife," he said, "don't you think it would be a good idea to stay up one night, and find out who is helping us?"

His wife agreed. So that night, instead of going to bed, they hid in the workroom and waited.

At midnight there was a sound of tiny feet, like the sound that mice make. But it wasn't mice that ran across the floor—it was two tiny men. They climbed up onto the workbench and set to work, with needles as big as themselves and reels of thread that were a lot bigger.

"Elves!" the shoemaker whispered. "Elves have been helping us."

"Poor little things," said his wife. "They haven't a stitch on. They must be cold. Husband, let's make them clothes!"

So the next day the shoemaker's wife went out and bought little pieces of the best velvets and silks she could find. All week long she cut and sewed, doing her best to make the finest little suits with the neatest little stitches. Little velvet jackets and breeches, tiny silk shirts and stockings she made, while the shoemaker used the softest leather to make tiny little shoes.

On Christmas Eve they finished the gifts, wrapped them up and left them on the workbench. Then they hid, to see what the elves would say when they found the presents.

At midnight, the elves ran across the floor and up onto the workbench. When they unwrapped the clothes, they put them on at once, and danced about admiring each other.

"Why, brother," said one elf, "we can't work at a greasy old shoemaker's bench in velvet and silk!"

"I shall never work again!" said the other. "Not now I'm so fine!" The two little elves jumped down from the workbench and ran away. They never came back.

But by now the shoemaker was so famous for his wonderful shoes that he still did good business. No one noticed that his stitches were not quite so tiny nor his seams so smooth, and he and his family were never poor again.

Brer Rabbit and the Tar-Baby

Foxes like eating rabbits, and Brer Fox had been trying, for a long time, to catch Brer Rabbit and eat him. But Brer Rabbit always managed to get away somehow, by one trick or another. It made Brer Fox mad.

Now Brer Fox was walking along the road one day, and he came across some tar that had been left there. It was a hot day, and the tar was soft and sticky in the sun. Brer Fox thought of a way he could use that sticky tar to catch Brer Rabbit.

Brer Fox got some twigs and covered them with sticky tar, and he made a sort of baby-shape. He stood it up by the side of the road, and then he went and hid himself in a bush. "You stand there, sticky tar-baby," said Brer Fox. "You wait for Brer Rabbit. He gets away from me, but he won't get away from you!"

After a while, along came Brer Rabbit, hopping and jumping with his tail stuck up behind him.

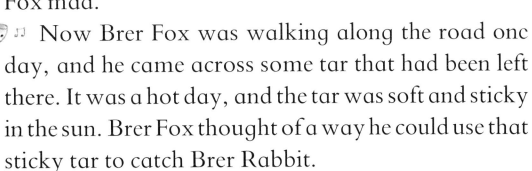

Brer Rabbit saw the tar-baby standing by the side of the road, and he called out, "Good morning to you!"

The tar-baby said nothing.

Well, Brer Rabbit thought the tar-baby hadn't heard him, so he went a bit closer and he spoke a bit louder. "Good morning!" he said. "It's a fine day."

The tar-baby said nothing.

"Are you deaf?" shouted Brer Rabbit. "I said 'Good morning' to you twice, and you just stand there saying nothing. Some folk would think that rude."

The tar-baby said nothing.

"Well, you sure are high and mighty," said Brer Rabbit. "When someone says 'Good morning' to you, it's polite to say 'Good morning' back. So let's hear you say it."

But the tar-baby said nothing.

Brer Rabbit was angry. "If you don't say 'Good morning', I'm going to let you have one right on the chin!"

The tar-baby still said nothing.

So Brer Rabbit punched the tar-baby right on the chin. But the tar-baby was sticky, and Brer Rabbit's paw stuck to the tar. No matter how Brer Rabbit pulled, he couldn't get his paw free.

"Let me go!" Brer Rabbit shouted, while Brer Fox laughed to himself in the bush nearby. "Let me go or I'll hit you with the other paw!"

But the tar-baby said nothing and didn't let Brer Rabbit go.

So Brer Rabbit hit the tar-baby as hard as he could with the other paw. And his other paw got stuck too. Now Brer Rabbit had both front paws stuck to the tar-baby, and he couldn't get loose, no matter how he struggled. "Let me go," said Brer Rabbit, "or I'll kick you!"

But the tar-baby didn't let him go.

So Brer Rabbit kicked the tar-baby, and got his foot stuck in the sticky tar, and couldn't get it loose. Then Brer Rabbit kicked the tar-baby with the other foot, and that got stuck too. So there was Brer Rabbit, with all four feet stuck in the tar, and he couldn't get loose, no matter how he struggled and yelled.

Then Brer Fox came out of his bush, laughing. "You think you're so clever," said Brer Fox, "but you're just a plain fool. I'm going to eat you, Brer Rabbit, and that'll be the end of you!"

"Oh," said Brer Rabbit, "cook me and eat me and I hope you enjoy me. That's not half as bad as what I thought you were going to do."

Brer Fox was puzzled.

"What did you think I was going to do?" he asked.

"Oh, it's too horrible," said Brer Rabbit.

"Tell me quick!" shouted Brer Fox.

"Oh, I thought you were going to throw me in the briar patch."

"Throwing you in the briar patch is worse than cooking and eating you?"

"Oh, yes!"

"Well then, I'll hang you from a tree," said Brer Fox. "That'll be worse than eating you."

"Hang me from a tree, cook me and eat me," said Brer Rabbit, "only please, please don't throw me in the briar patch!"

"Then I'll drown you!" said Brer Fox. "*That'll* be worse than eating you!"

"Oh, drown me, please drown me," said Brer Rabbit. "Drown me, then hang me, then cook me and eat me, so long as you don't throw me in that terrible briar patch."

"Then I *will* throw you in the briar patch!" said Brer Fox, and he tore Brer Rabbit off the tar-baby and threw him right into the middle of the briar patch. "There!" shouted Brer Fox. "Serves you right, Brer Rabbit!"

But not a sound came from Brer Rabbit in the briar patch. Brer Fox stopped and listened. Then he heard singing—Brer Rabbit *singing* in the briar patch!

This is the song:

"I was born and bred in a briar patch, Brer Fox!
Thorns'll never hurt me, Brer Fox!
I've lived all my life in a briar patch, Brer Fox!
I'm right where I want to be, Brer Fox!"

So Brer Rabbit tricked Brer Fox and got away, again! Brer Fox sneaked off and didn't dare show his face for a good many days. All the rabbits would have laughed at him if he had.

And that's the end of the story—but it was a good one while it lasted.

The Enormous Turnip

Once upon a time there was an old man who planted a turnip seed in the ground and waited for it to grow.

First it grew into a small turnip, then a middling turnip, then a big turnip, then a bigger turnip, and then an enormous turnip! The old man decided that it was time to pull the turnip up and eat it.

So he took hold of the turnip and pulled. But the turnip stayed in the ground.

The old man took a better grip and pulled harder. The turnip still stayed in the ground.

Then the old man gritted his teeth and pulled and pulled and pulled, until he had no pull left in him. But the turnip stayed in the ground.

So the old man went to his wife and said, "Wife, come and help me pull up this turnip."

So the old woman went with him back to the turnip. She took hold of the old man, the old man took hold of the turnip and they pulled. They pulled again.

They pulled and they pulled and they pulled, until they had no pull left in them. And the turnip stayed in the ground.

So the old woman went and found her granddaughter and said, "Granddaughter, come and help us pull up this turnip!"

The granddaughter went back with the old woman. She took hold of the old woman, the old woman took hold of the old man, the old man took hold of the turnip and they got ready. "Now let's try tugging," said the old man.

So they tugged.

They TUGGED and they TUGGED and they TUGGED, until none of them had any tug left. And the turnip stayed in the ground.

So the granddaughter went and found the dog. "Dog," she said, "come and help us tug this turnip up." The dog went with the girl back to the turnip.

The dog took hold of the girl, the girl took hold of the old woman, the old woman took hold of the old man, the old man took hold of the turnip, and they all got ready. "Let's try heaving," said the old man.

So they heaved at the turnip.

They HEAVED, and they HEAVED, and they HEAVED.

HEAVE . . .

HEAVE . . .

HEAVE . . . until none of them had any heave left in them. And the turnip stayed in the ground.

So the dog went away and found the cat and said, "Cat, come and help us heave up this turnip."

The cat went with the dog, and took hold of the dog. The dog took hold of the girl, the girl took hold of the old woman, the old woman took hold of the old man, the old man took hold of the turnip, and they all got ready. "Let's try dragging it this time."

So they dragged at the turnip.

They dragged again.

And the turnip came up out of the ground!

And the cat fell on the ground, the dog fell on the cat, the girl fell on the dog, the old woman fell on her granddaughter and the old man fell on his wife, and the turnip fell on the old man.

It took all of them to pull, tug, heave, and drag the turnip to the house. There they cut it up and made it into turnip soup. There was more than enough for everyone, and for all I know, the old man, the old woman, their granddaughter, the dog, and the cat have lived on turnip soup from that day to this, and are all eating huge bowlfuls of turnip soup this very minute, even as you are listening to this story.

But that's enough of turnips, and the end of the story.

Little Red Riding Hood

Once upon a time, there was a dark forest, where wolves and bears lived. It was easy to get lost in that forest.

Close to the forest lived a poor woodcutter and his wife. They had one little girl, and they loved her very much. They called her Little Red Riding Hood, because she always wore a hooded cloak that her Granny had made for her. It was as red as poppies or holly berries.

Little Red Riding Hood's Granny lived on the other side of the forest. One day, Little Red Riding Hood's mother put some cakes and bread into a basket and said, "Little Red Riding Hood, take these things through the forest to your Granny. But make sure you keep to the path, so that you don't get lost. And don't stop to talk to *anyone*. Go straight there and come straight back."

"I will," said Little Red Riding Hood.

She set off through the dark forest, in her bright red cloak and hood, carrying the basket. She hadn't gone very far when she saw some flowers growing by the path. She decided to pick some for her Granny. Then she saw some bigger, prettier flowers growing among the trees, and she left the path to pick them as well.

While she was picking flowers, a wolf came by.

"Good day, Little Red Riding Hood," said the wolf. "How are you?"

Little Red Riding Hood said, "I'm very well, thank you. How are you?"

"I'm as well as can be expected when I'm so hungry," said the wolf. "That basket looks heavy. Where are you taking it?"

"I'm taking some food to my Granny," said Little Red Riding Hood.

The wolf licked his chops. "If I'm clever," he thought, "I'll be able to eat this little girl *and* her Granny." So he said, "It'll take you a long time to get to your Granny's if you follow that twisty path. I know a shortcut through the trees. Come with me and I'll show you."

"No, I can't come with you, and I'd better go back to the path," said Little Red Riding Hood. "My mother told me not to leave the path. You shouldn't ever leave the path when you are in the forest. Don't you know that, wolf?"

"Oh, you'll be safe with me," said the wolf. "Come along."

"No," said Little Red Riding Hood, and she went back to the path, with her basket and her flowers.

"Never mind," thought the wolf. "I'll just run ahead to her Granny's and wait for her there."

And off he ran through the trees. Little Red Riding Hood went on her way along the path.

But the way through the trees was shorter, so the wolf reached Granny's house first.

He knocked on the door with his paw. From inside, Granny called, "Who's there?"

The wolf made his voice sweet and soft and gentle, as wolves can when they want to. "It's your granddaughter, Little Red Riding Hood, come to see you."

"Then lift up the latch and walk in," Granny called.

But when the door opened, in came the hungry forest wolf, and ate Granny up.

The wolf licked his chops, and dressed himself in Granny's nightdress and nightcap, and climbed into Granny's bed. He pulled the bedclothes right up to his chin and waited for Little Red Riding Hood.

Little Red Riding Hood came up the forest path to Granny's house and knocked on the door. From inside came a soft, sweet, gentle voice: "Who's there?"

"It's me, Granny!" said Little Red Riding Hood.

"Then lift up the latch and walk in."

Little Red Riding Hood opened the door and went in.

Little Red Riding Hood stood at the end of
Granny's bed and said, "Oh Granny, what big eyes
you have!"

"All the better to see you with," said the wolf.

"Oh, but Granny, what big ears you have!"

"All the better to hear you with."

"Oh, but Granny, what big teeth you have!"

"All the better to eat you with!" said the wolf and jumped out of bed. Off fell the nightdress, off fell the nightcap, and Little Red Riding Hood saw that it was not Granny but the wolf! She hit the wolf with her basket and shouted for help as loudly as she could.

Outside in the forest, Little Red Riding Hood's father was at work, chopping wood. He heard Little Red Riding Hood shouting and ran to see what the matter was. When he opened the door, he saw Little Red Riding Hood fighting with the wolf. With one blow of his ax, he cut off the wolf's head, and out came Granny! She hugged and kissed Little Red Riding Hood, and hugged and kissed Little Red Riding Hood's father.

And Little Red Riding Hood never talked to wolves or left the path again.

Rumpelstiltskin

There was once a woman who baked nine pies and put them in her pantry to cool while she went to fetch water. When she came back, she found that her daughter had eaten all nine pies!

"Well!" said the woman. And to tease her daughter she made up a song:

"My daughter ate nine pies today!

My daughter ate nine pies today!"

As she was singing, the King rode by on his way to the castle. He stopped and said, "What was that you were singing?"

The woman blushed; she was ashamed to admit that her daughter was so greedy. So she said, "Oh Sire, I was just singing that my daughter spun nine skeins today."

"Nine skeins?" said the King. "Very good."

"Yes Sire," the woman boasted. "And they were all gold!"

"Nine *gold* skeins?" said the King.

"Yes, and she spun them from straw!"

"Straw into gold!" exclaimed the King. "Where is your daughter? I shall marry her at once."

The woman fetched her daughter out of the house, and the King took her straight to his castle and married her that very day.

The girl was wonderfully happy at being married to the King. She was Queen, and could have anything she wanted—a gold ring, a gold necklace, pretty dresses, anything.

But, three days after the wedding, the King took her to a room at the top of a stone tower.

The room was filled with bales of straw. There was nothing else in the room at all, except a stool and a spinning wheel.

"I need some gold for my treasury," said the King. "Spin this straw into gold, wife."

The girl was terrified. "I might not be able to spin *all* this straw into gold, Sire . . ."

"All of it," said the King. "By tomorrow morning, or I'll chop off your head!" And out he went, locking the door behind him. The poor girl sat down on the stool and cried.

Then a voice said, "Tears won't spin straw into gold, but I can."

81

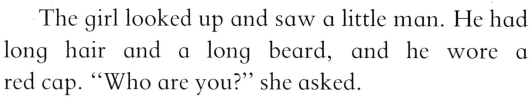

The girl looked up and saw a little man. He had long hair and a long beard, and he wore a red cap. "Who are you?" she asked.

"Never mind who I am. Do you want my help?"

"Oh, yes please!" said the girl.

"What will you give me?" asked the little man.

"I'll give you this gold ring," said the girl. She pulled the ring off her finger and held it out to him.

"That will do," he said, and he sat down at the spinning wheel and started to spin. The girl sat on a straw bale and watched him work. Soon he needed the bale she was sitting on, so she sat on a pile of gold thread instead. Long before morning every bit of straw had been spun into gold. The little man got up off the stool, jumped out of the window and was gone.

When the King unlocked the door a few hours later, he was delighted with all his gold. But he wanted more. The next night, he took the girl to the

same room, with an even bigger pile of straw.

"Now, spin the whole lot into gold by morning," he said, "—or I'll chop off your head!" And out he went, locking the door behind him.

The girl began to cry again. But again the little man appeared.

"What will you give me this time?" he asked.

"My necklace," said the girl.

"That will do," said the little man. He sat down at the spinning wheel and long before morning he had spun every scrap of straw into gold thread. Away through the window he went, with the Queen's necklace.

When the King saw the roomful of gold in the morning, he said, "Just once more, wife, and we shall have enough gold to last us for ever." He had the room filled with straw and left, locking the door behind him.

The girl was sure the little man would come again, and so he did.

"What will you give me this time?" he asked.

"I have no more rings or necklaces," said the girl. "But do the spinning and tomorrow I'll be able to pay you anything you like."

"Tomorrow's no good to me," the little man said. "We must fix a price tonight."

"What would you like?"

The little man grinned. "I would like," he said, "your first-born child. Promise!"

Well, the Queen had no children, so she didn't think this was much to promise. "All right," she said. "I promise: my first-born child shall be yours."

The little man sat down at the spinning wheel and set to work. By morning the room was full of gleaming gold thread. "Remember your promise!" said the little man, and leaped out of the window.

At last the King was happy. "No more spinning," he said. Now the girl could enjoy being Queen again. In fact, as time went by she was so busy enjoying herself that she forgot all about the little man and the promise she had made.

She was happier still when, a year later, her first baby was born. But that night, as she lay in bed with her baby in its cradle beside her, the little man with the long hair and beard and the red cap jumped in through the window.

"Here I am! I've come to fetch my baby!"

The Queen snatched her baby from the cradle.

"Have you forgotten your promise?" said the little man. "The baby is mine."

"No!" cried the Queen. "You can have anything else, but not my baby."

"I don't want anything else," said the little man. "Only the baby."

The Queen knelt and pleaded with the little man. He seemed to feel sorry for her, because he said, "I will let you keep your baby, on one condition ... You must guess my name. I'll give you three days, but if you can't guess, you must give me the baby. Do you agree to that?"

"Oh yes, yes!" said the Queen. She knew she had no choice.

"Guess away then."

The Queen sat down on the edge of her bed, with her baby in her arms. She began to try to guess the little man's name.

"Is your name Peter?" she asked.

"No," said the little man.

"Is it Hans?"

"No."

"Is it David?"

"No."

On and on the guessing went, all night long, but to all the Queen's guesses the little man answered, "No." When morning came he leaped out of the window.

The Queen called together all the cleverest people in the Kingdom, and asked them to write down all the boys' names they could think of. In case there were names even those clever people didn't know, she also sent messengers to every part of the Kingdom, to find out and write down the names of every man they met.

When the little man came back on the second

night, the Queen had sheets and sheets of paper by her side, with hundreds of names written on them.

"Well, Queen, do you know my name yet?" the little man asked.

"Is it Lucius?" said the Queen, reading from her list.

"No."

"Augustus?"

"No."

"Marcus?"

"No."

All through the second night, the guessing game went on and on, until morning came and the little man disappeared.

On the third morning the messengers came back to the castle with more lists. "It must be one of these names," the Queen said to herself, "it must be."

It was growing dark when the youngest messenger rode into the courtyard, and ran breathlessly up the stairs to see the Queen.

"Your Majesty, as I was riding through a dark forest I saw a fire. When I came close, I saw a little man dancing around the fire."

"Did he have long hair and a long beard, and a red cap?" asked the Queen.

"Yes, Your Majesty. And as he danced, he sang, and this is what he sang:

'First I brew, then I bake,

Tomorrow the Queen's child I'll take;

At guessing my name she'll never win,

For it is RUMPELSTILTSKIN!' "

"Rumpelstiltskin!" said the Queen. "Is that a name?"

"It's the strangest name I've ever heard," said the messenger, "but that is what he sang."

The Queen rewarded the boy with a precious ring, and waited for the little man.

He appeared, grinning. "One last chance, Queen," he said. "And when you can't guess my name, I shall take away my baby!"

"Oh!" said the Queen, pretending to be afraid. "Is your name Finn?"

"No." And the little man grinned again.

"Is it Jerome?"

"No." And the little man laughed.

The sun was coming up and the sky began to grow lighter. The little man leaned over the baby's cradle.

"Is it—is it Rumpelstiltskin?"

The little man stood with his mouth open. "Yes," he said.

"Then I keep my baby!" said the Queen. The little man flung down his cap in rage, leaped from the window and was never seen again.

And that is the end of the story, except to say that the Queen and her baby lived happily ever after and the Queen named her baby—guess what?

The Princess and the Pea

Once upon a time there was a Prince, and he wanted to marry a Princess; but she had to be a *real* Princess. He traveled all over the world in his search for a Princess, and Princesses he found in plenty; but whether they were *real* Princesses he couldn't decide, for now one thing, now another, seemed not quite right. At last he returned home to his palace and was very sad, because he wished so much to have a real Princess for his wife.

One evening there was a fearful storm; thunder crashed, lightning flashed, rain poured down from the sky in torrents—and it was dark as dark as can be. All at once there was heard a knocking at the door. The Prince's father, the old King himself, went out to open it.

A Princess stood outside; but gracious! what a sight she was, out there in the rain. Water trickled down from her hair; water dripped from her clothes; water ran in at the toes of her shoes and out at the heels. And yet she said she was a real Princess.

"We shall soon see about that!" thought the old Queen, but she didn't say anything.

She went into the bedroom, took all the clothes off the bed and laid one dried pea on the mattress. Then she piled twenty more mattresses on top of it, and

twenty eiderdowns over that. On this the girl who said she was a real Princess was to lie all night.

The next morning she was asked how she had slept.

"Oh, shockingly!" she replied. "I haven't even closed my eyes. I don't know what was in my bed, but there was something hard that has bruised me all over."

They saw at once that she must be a *real* Princess, for she had felt the little dried pea through twenty eiderdowns and twenty mattresses. Only a *real* Princess could have such delicate skin.

So the Prince asked the Princess to marry him, and the pea was put in a museum, as a curiosity. You may go yourself and see it.

Now, wasn't that a *real* story?